Lost, Hurt, or in Transit Beautiful

I sincerely hope that *Lost, Hurt, or in Transit Beautiful* will find many readers. Why? Because Rohan Chhetri is a real poet. What does it mean, in these days of easy praise, to say that someone is 'a real poet'? For me, it means this is a person who hears that 'clean music of bones'. Someone who can speak in tongues and yet make sense of 'how we arrive / at clarity'. In other words: someone whose linguistic ability is inimitable. Chhetri is that kind of poet, yes. The textures of his language are undeniably beautiful. But there is more. He is someone who knows how to take a personal story and make it into a myth that will last. This is a poet who can take any landscape, say 'land blistered by drought & the blight of small towns' and by just speaking of it make it memorable. This is a poet who can take a character and by just describing that character's motion give it something indelible: 'he rides pillion on the old scooter singing / because the breeze makes him young in the face.' This book has pain and it has discovery. It has wonder. It has the spell of a story and the effortlessness of a song. Which is why I hope it finds its way into your hands, readers.

—ILYA KAMINSKY, author of *Deaf Republic*

To read Rohan Chhetri's poetry is to be ever-astonished—struck by the 'clean music of bones', the glimpse of a childhood friend in an old face like a 'vertiginous drop down the cool dark of an abandoned well', of day 'dimly lit by the shadow of a blown out sun', by 'thirst in the shape of a deer'. This is poetry peopled by ancestors, restless 'giants walking the earth', whose histories drip through the pages like blood, like tears, situated in childhood place, the small town, the youth clubhouse turned army encampment, fields after rain, rent by atrocities and revolution. Memory echoes like a temple bell, but Chhetri's is not the poetry of simple remembrance or nostalgia—rather it seethes with life of the moment, with movement, whether through cities, old and new, on trains, through desire, and ambition, arriving always at a startling unexpected elsewhere. Sometimes rent, destroyed, broken, yet always, always tender. *Lost, Hurt, or in Transit Beautiful* reads raw and honest, vulnerable and true—'Once you crawl white-eyed through a field of bones into light, what happens next?' a poem asks, and I wish to say this, only this.

—JANICE PARIAT, author of *The Nine-Chambered Heart*

This is a searing book, its imagery in turns gruesome and gorgeous, its language utterly riveting… His poems deliver an arresting vision of lives overfilled with anguish and sorrow, and yet somehow, in the exquisite craftedness of this work, beauty persists. In all, *Lost, Hurt, or in Transit Beautiful* does exactly what poetry books are meant to do: it alters the mind. And I am forever grateful for it.

—JASWINDER BOLINA, author of *Of Color* and *Phantom Camera*

Praise for *Slow Startle*

Gifted with lyric intensity… Chhetri suggests familiarity rather than knowledge, for he admits to the presence of strangeness… [He] is not interested in raising ontological questions but rather in producing affect that takes readers to the heart of the human condition.

—*New Orleans Review*, MANASH FIRAQ BHATTACHARJEE,
author of *The Town Slowly Empties*

Everything is at stake here, in sentences that dazzle and console. I don't know how else to say it—read this book.

—JEET THAYIL, author of *These Errors Are Correct* and *Names of the Women*

Lost, Hurt, or in Transit Beautiful

poems

ROHAN CHHETRI

HarperCollins *Publishers* India

First published in India in 2021 by
HarperCollins *Publishers*
A-75, Sector 57, Noida, Uttar Pradesh 201301, India
www.harpercollins.co.in

2 4 6 8 10 9 7 5 3 1

P-ISBN: 978-93-5422-427-0
E-ISBN: 978-93-5422-428-7

Typeset in 11.5/16.5 Arno Pro at
Manipal Technologies Limited, Manipal

Printed and bound at
Replika Press Pvt. Ltd.

FSC www.fsc.org MIX Paper from responsible sources FSC® C016779

This book is produced from independently certified FSC® paper to ensure responsible forest management.

'If down there they ever talk about such things,
if they can be bothered with the like at all.'

C.P. Cavafy, 'The Rest I'll Speak of to the Ones Below in Hades',
trans. Seamus Heaney

'A place of first permission,
everlasting omen of what is.'

Robert Duncan, 'Often I Am Permitted to Return to a Meadow'

'Only like can write about like. Only the dead can write about the dead. But the dead are very feeble.'

Augusto Roa Bastos, *I the Supreme*
trans. Helen Lane

Contents

Erato

Grief Deer

Katabasis

King's Feedery

After the rape & the bloodbath, the savage king
& his men retired to a long shed built in an open
field by a thin river fashioned for this lull in the pillaging
so the horses could rest. One by one, they scrubbed
blood off their fingers & faces & sat down to devour
a feast of rice & goat served by the villagers.
The legend remains only in the name of a lodge
built in the same place, which from the Bengali means
the King's Feedery, where the king took his meal.
We say Death stays here when it visits someone
in the family. The time it came for Grandfather, it arrived
late. Not at the wolf's hour between midnight & first
light, but late morning on the highway, siren blaring
all the way to the nursing home. As if punishing us
for what it botched, it hung around for a few
months at the Feedery, then came for my aunt. Young,
suffering in a marriage, she was taken straight by her weak
heart. I imagine them, father & daughter, sitting still
across a table, sharing a meal of steaming boiled potatoes,
& always in the afterlife that vague dream of salt.
Death takes in threes, they said. We feared it would
come for one of us. In the trashed room,
they found Death's ledger full of illegible scrawls
in a dark meter no one could understand.
Grandmother's devastation circled complete, that year
a channel of clear water began thrumming beneath
her skin. We heard it rumble whenever she opened

her mouth to speak. When I think of love,
I think of her weeping as I left, her swollen lip
grazing the back of my hand through the car window. Brief
& bright her long blurred life now summoned
with Death lurking at the borders again.
Married at thirteen, adolescence lost
weeping into a cauldron of chopped onions. She talks
of the flimsy wooden hovel perched on four
frayed stumps & in her telling it is always
how she saw it first, herself decked in gold
with that sinking dread: a preface. I think of love
& I think how when they lifted Grandfather's bier
she called out to him crying *My child*
my god   *my child*

The Singing Bone

The shaman comes to the valley after midnight
Circling our boarding house. Pinned to our small beds
In terror, we listen to the clean music of bones.
Later, through a rift in the curtain, we squint into the mist
But cannot see the past from a man
Blowing the trumpet of a suicide's hollow shinbone.

Twenty years will pass before I understand this music
Robbed from a grave. Sleepless in the new world,
Listening to the laboring salt trucks make rounds
On the frozen streets, it will come back to me
All at once: the echo chamber of the creaking bamboo
Grove where we smoked our first cigarette,

The army of deaf and mute in the village who spoke
Only in obscene gestures, the lonely daughter
From the herbarium who wrote letters to us
In a hen's scrawl. The old house replaced
By something modern, architecture standing in
For a woman's death. Her husband's slow breakdown

Coursed for months, the clocks telling him to jump
Off a cliff, the second marriage hurried in mourning.
The white seed of lunacy sleeps, then swells to its fate.
But all our fears of summer snakes & rabid dogs,
Everything depended on them granting us safe passage
Through fields redolent with the smell of semen

After a night of rain. Caught in the downpour,
We stood under eaves of caves. The wind churned,
Some vegetation pushed up lightless from the silver-blue
Mud. We hollowed hovels out of lantana brambles
Where we spoke in the voices of already grown men.
In winter, I traveled down as the coiling roads of the world

Grew dark. I held my insides, bile-soaked, where joy
Trembled. Prospect of home washed in the retch
Of anxiety. My history of nausea in the cold half-
Light of childhood, where did it come from? Mother,
Or the long descent in the old manner of hell—
The asphalt frozen, slippery all the way home.

The shaman returns the next morning for alms,
Turmeric, rice, strip of black cloth. We circle him,
The mystification undone in daylight. Just a man bruised
From the cold, with children starving somewhere
In the mountains across the border, as we sit here
Goading him to reveal to us the singing bone.

Lamentation for a Failed Revolution

This poem derives its antiphonal structure loosely from the Moirolói and the ritual lament tradition in ancient Greek.

৩.৫

—long summer of bullets
One July morning   a caesura in the terror a lull
in the pelting   A man woke in the shape of a crosshair
looking for a pharmacy   He heard it before he—
White blow above ear then blank   then black
blood sluicing down an eye   His open mouth vacuum-
still on the incline of a sidewalk   fistful of pipelines
twisting into the asphalt   beside his head his
hand clutching dust   body splayed fossil-ripe
martyring

১

The autocrat was a small woman in white
with old stitch marks on her head.
On the TV we heard a speech about time
having come to replace our tongues.
We will start with your children, she said.
It will be painless. We'll bring our best.
It was an appendage
they wanted to sew into our little ones
while the low vaults of their mouths were still
busy with the simple underswell
of small hurt and hunger.

𑇑

I sat at home paralyzed   On TV blared
their newsrooms   gagged ours boarded nailed
shut I watched *The Turin Horse*   that horse manifesting
a dumb mutiny   in a world about to go still
Winter of 1986:
Grandfather home after   a week in the lock-up
hung by the feet baton-blued   calves taste of dirt
black he could never spit out   His quietness:
      A tall house with the wiring   blown no word
about the revolution   We speak only of his quietness
after
    The long rich hours of his sleep

𑇒

One morning the troops swarmed into town
like ants around spilled tea. Weary and hungry,
they stormed our hearths. We fed them.
They were starved, they'd traveled so far.
The trials began the following night. They dragged
our children's fathers down to the river.
Held them by the hair, pulled their tongues
out of their mouths taut like catgut.
Some looked embarrassed. So young some of them.
One cracked a joke. They all laughed.
Be still, someone whispered. The river raved
and raved eating up the moaning
turning hollow in our mouths.

Another afternoon   a fifteen-year-old boy
Hear the bullet   thud to breast like second heart
pain's rubbery percussion   the way he looked up
mouth a shucked-oyster wobble   Alive
in the elongating horror   A nurse dressing a medieval coin-
sized chunk of skin   fallen off the areola
where a round   radiating wound his mother
beside him beside herself   *you're lucky they didn't*
shoot you with lead   Every failed revolution is a child
learning the edge of himself   Every revolution is a child
grown before fire

First, the soldiers thought the roaring
came from within the river, some force
answering the fog. Then they saw us, the widening
pack of us moving through trees. They dropped
their guns, scurried to the barracks downtown.
Next morning we woke and we brushed and braided
each other's hair and we marched and we had no choice.
Low humming in the streets at first,
then fire, soot, blood darkening asphalt,
shards of tube lights, flaring car bonnets. Overnight
the hills grown with eyes with teeth with target.

8

One morning we woke   to the coughing
vampire in a child's body   century old
smelling of taxidermy & treaty   bad memory
teething   bloodthirst one morning we woke
it was the revolution   again season of ash-
men bone & flesh   before that cool mornings
humid afternoons long   evening's brief monsoon
march through power cuts they   made love
as electrocuted crows   smoked above power lines
Before that   I will not name them
I want their deaths to be meaningless
full of rest

9

Soon we understood what we were
up against, an unfathomable hatred.
They hated us just like they hated those others,
like we hated those others.
The butchers, the untouchables … We imagined
we were better. They'll treat us better,
we thought. Our infants wailed in hunger
as the first bodies began to fall. Someone said
they are shooting us only in the faces.
The holes in our temples opened
into an abandoned factory yard
where our dead sat around a bonfire of flags.

൪

No lord   in the torched kingdom
we heard in the town zoo the animals
A shirtless man   self-immolated
howled curses up a hill   as his comrades chased
beating him   down with coat-tails trying to douse
the flames swarming his face   Trail of paint-
thick blood on the rained   streets where they dragged
two baby red pandas were born in captivity on the twenty-ninth
day of the curfew we named them   bodies falling
through crossfire   smoke tear-gas shells
bullets plunked from   the hands of twenty-year-olds
brought up in the hard   streets of small towns
just like ours   Given guns first then made
                    to be afraid of us

Sebastian

'As if this were the thing the other had to learn and he to teach' Gilgamesh

On a cold concrete bench, he sat, high
as a sloth, outside a monastery in Phuentsholing
gazing at the light through treetops.
Dim-eyed monks around him rehearsed
their ancient prayers in a language that excludes
themselves, & hence, is now rote, manifesto.
        Improbable music, my friend,
when I put my hand on your shoulder, you took
your time training your red eyes on mine
& something inside you flickered.
I remembered the last melodramatic dispatch
that embarrassed you to oblivion.
        For so long I felt he was dead
or so alive I couldn't bring myself to imagine
his ruined light, & yet here he was, grinning,
the old boy so far inside him, just looking
into his face was a vertiginous drop down
the cool dark of an abandoned well, & him
a thin shade at the bottom among the bones.

The last of the mother lovers, my friend Sebastian,
whose Ma kissed him on the mouth before bed
until he was sixteen, to sniff for glue on his breath,
& him petrified to go home on days
we blew our hunger into the blank cave
of a polythene bag until its insides glazed

like our small lit hearts. Who kept kissing
my battered feet on the football field until
the paramedics arrived while I howled
in pain. Old man in a child's body, my friend
Sebastian, whose soul grew inside an eighth-
grader's ribcage for life.

Running the obstacle race agile as a field
mouse maneuvering a harvest. His epic
imitations of the great wrestlers of our day,
his melancholy, & the truth about himself
always a little less or more than his claims,
as if to look at oneself & speak truly
would destroy one down to the soul.

The school's prize midfielder
who never graduated from the junior team,
the star sprinter who once stood at the finishing
line, bent over, breathless, trying to sever
with his tongue the blood-laced sputum
trailing from the corner of his mouth. Already
the fumes beginning to cut through his insides.

Dear Sebastian, coming home from the airport
today, I saw a lone truck loaded with river boulders
trapped in a flash flood & the driver still
inside, trying to clamber his way out towards
the hood, while the shit-colored water wrested
out of a dam had begun rushing in, filling
the dashboard & gears, & I never saw him
emerging from it, for the taxi I was in
had somewhere to get to & drove calmly on.
I thought of you, chasing the tail of the gray
dragon all the way down to the mossy bottom

of that well, how many days now, water dried
up to your ankles & against the round bright air
above, a silhouette: mine.

Me, I wanted to say, friend, as you took
my hand off your shoulder like brushing off
a small unease, & I took it for insult. I walked out,
indignant, cursing under my breath. You should've
seen me, hurrying out into the fading light
as if my life depended on it. As if to save
someone was to enter the flash flood, to battle
the dragon with the two purple wisps of fumes
for fangs, to bring my own self to safety first,
just to see if it could be done at all.

The Indian Railway Canticle

Three days two nights in a metal box laddering
down the barren heartland of the republic.
Land blistered by drought & the blight of small towns:
religion, fratricide, mass-distributed snuff films
in the paan shops. I was a boy trying to get home,
the city flinging me out. For hours I read
L'Étranger, counted the mullions on the windows,
pushed my feet against the warm breathing
wall of aluminium & sunmica, drifting in a heat
induced slumber on the upper berth where
the hijra couldn't reach over & pinch my cock. Outside,
the precision of metal & wheels: long blue
metaphor of the wandering womb in transit. I saw
storms lash the rice fields, lightning bolts
brighter than all the village's light bulbs put together.
The sun bearing down infernal since dawn,
breathing fissures into the earth. So why not the sorrow
farmer sowing himself in the crosshairs
of the oncoming train. I've seen in kinder times
the freight cars grind to a halt to let a herd
of elephants pass. That one time outside the train
window: a young woman in a niqab & a ferret-
faced infant on her hips yanking her hair with still
the blind rage of birth. No hope for it,
we saw the brooding swine of a father. The men
in the compartment looked on, disbelieving at first,
jealous of the idiot taking her home, then all at once

saddened by her beauty. Apologists for the low-
grade genocide lost for words. The train moved along,
into the evening we nursed that silence to sleep
& all night the urinous stink moved in the compartments
like an old ghost. The shed & filth cumulating
in the cars by the day's end. The food, the flying spices,
language changing every hundred kilometers.
Outside, the elements beating down on the trundling
worm of rust, the landscape fuzzing across state
lines, airborne viral strains, the dim industry with its sewer
breath at night to the fragrant mist rising off harvest
hay in the morning. Closer home, I saw a deer stray
along the edge of the monsoon's verdure. I saw
disappeared children made to beg in the arms of the crippled.
I met hucksters who tried to offer me tea with ketamine.
A leper radiating the same diameter of horror
as the untouchable. I heard a couple make love
inside a coarse blanket on the upper berth. Then arriving
home, always the bruised sky of dawn telling me
something I knew, for a moment, then didn't.

Locus Amoenus

Bordersong

We lived downwind of a bakery,
butter sesame roasted black cumin.

From a mosque downwind drifted prayer
erasing the gummy hour of the wolf,
sleepy holler of a child muezzin.

We lived downwind of a temple. Incense,
synonymous with the clear earache of a gong
haloing a bell's rim before withering to the ground.

Downwind of a cremation ghat, incense,
                                    another kind: cloying, rot-sweet,
burning flesh masked in clarified butter woodsmoke hunger
                all synonyms for the Lord's true name.

From the butcher shop, downwind musk of flensed pelt,
shit-gutted intestines, opaque green eyes on severed goat heads.

Downwind we lived too of the army barracks, once
a youth club, our lost tennis tables moonlighting
for the feast of soldiers.
            In the night fragrant with the tea gardens' first flush
we heard the pain-astonished men thrashing upside down
as a baton tore welts into their calves.

Our tall house stood downwind of a peaceful kingdom's border.
Odor of fermented betelnut. What the Rimpoche once
bestowed to the cannibals in lieu of their blood-
rimmed thirst & craving of gnawbone.
    Then one night, truck after stealth-green
truck full of families packed to the hull
like horses for the New World.

Downwind of the grimy brothels in the border town
we visited as boys, petrified we would run
into our own fathers.
        Smell of talcum & attar
that bloomed at nightfall & withered by dawn
on a long Bhutanese street called Chinese Line.

All the nameless villages in between blurred
in the nightly music that blared from loudspeakers
to scare the elephants marauding the fields.

Downwind of the two severed heads of the Liberation
Front leaders hung from a branch of a guava tree
in the putrid summer of the old revolution.
                The women marched in gunmetal silence:
torches blinking in the rain, rhyme of slogans
plucked from their cleaved tongues.

Downwind blew kerosene & ragsmoke
in some young martyr's evening.

Fish Cross the Border in Rain

To go down to the river with my father.
He rides pillion on the old scooter singing
because the breeze makes him young in the face.
The dam thrown open in the kingdom
across the border the old aqueduct pulsing
gray slither of silt & gravel torn from gorges
where men wear lead batteries around their necks
and wade chest-deep casting low voltage
discs of current rounding the fish belly up.
To stand on the wave-nipped bank as shoal
after stunned shoal heave their nets. The fish
wake older dreaming brief new lives huddled
in a foreign prison gasping at each other's
gills blinded like a sack of mirrors.

Father, Farther: 1986

'Feed him the land, that is what they're fighting for'

Evening raid on a day I don't exist yet

It is hot as a crucible my grandfather is

dragged out of the house arrested

for possessing illicit maps of the new

state for harboring a party of separatist

leaders who sit smoking evenings

in our teahouse biding headcounts

of the vanished Across the border my mother

hurries my father to the market for salt

to make dinner On the way he meets the man

he reports to at the Army Welfare Project

who insists on buying my father a drink

Meanwhile my mother's waiting

begins & in her wait a blue chasm opens

Opens to where her father-in-law his feet
noose-tied through a ceiling fan hook
yanked upside down is stripped naked
water-boarded pummeled in the chest
in the stomach Later they'll feed him
fresh shoveled earth until it plugs
his windpipe until he cannot spit
soil can only will himself unconscious
as the taste grows familiar Like all men
who've seen death come walking
on bare hands my grandfather dreams
a long bright dream he is wincing in
as his eldest daughter cleans the caked
blood off his eyelids with alcohol

With alcohol the more he drinks
my father is farther away from dinner
from my mother waiting in the small
unheated quarter-house how she moves
in front of a tall mirror touches the bindi
in place & something else— reaches for
a sound of me in her womb I am
not there yet— swept floors of her sorrow
the aftersigh not me but her firstborn
stilled on arrival And my father now
begins to tell a story to the man
who asks *What are you people*
making a fuss about *a new state*
Look he whispers *this country of savages*

Savages & us   *sitting here warming*

our bellies with their brandy   *us honest men*

from two countries   One thing

he won't tell my father   the other

my father won't correct why   the ladder

for men like him   is designed sideways why

they are two men   honest hardly but

from the same nation   state of famine

& floodsong   Instead my father feels

a need to go further   back here he is

telling another drunk   about the time

he was a little boy staking   out acres of land

against armed policemen   in the middle

of a teeming   forest with my grandfather

Grandfather herding my young grandmother
my father five years old & the eldest daughter
to the jungle instructing all men to bring
their own so the police won't resort
to beating & blinding this land they'd been
clearing for a month & how on the ninth
day the daughter vomited the fever
black as the damp night fell asleep
in her & never woke My father remembers
the bloated belly her thirteen-year-old
body thrashing long hair & pale
skin flaking in the heat My father meant
to make a point through this *his* story
but he's drunk & the changkhang shutters

The shutters come down   two a.m.

my father stutters   uphill coat folded

over shoulder   Mother waiting on

a wicker chair outside   dew softening the hem

of her petticoat cold   rage turning her

white   & that moment Grandfather's

eyes blink open   tears have rivered down

his forehead in a pool of red   on the floor

he's been weeping   in the soil-dark

sleep of the bats   Now bewildered

awake his chest breaks   a ground-

swell of black horses   as he remembers

he's sent him   slow son across the border

where rifle barrels calcify   in the long rust of evening

National Grief

After L. Cohen

We grew heavier not with grief but numbers
as if we had suddenly become aware of the air
we stood in. As if we had only walked

lightly in a dream before. We heard
on the news a man had trekked seven hours across
the war-torn border into Aleppo to smuggle

toys for the children, so they could play
inside a bomb shelter. Someone heard
the mad sultan's ghost weeping

near the old mausoleum in Delhi, the day
a man died in a stampede outside a bank.
In a lab in Berlin, scientists tickled rats

till they giggled to their little deaths.
One morning in early November, stunned
silence sealed the air of fall, as if

some brute had risen to power. Nervous
laughter broke in corridors & all day yellow
leaves emptied aspens in a feverish spell.

A man drew a knife inside a city bus
as the thick snow curtained the world outside
in a vast white of indifference. The quiet

that followed, unlike the one that settles after
the barbarians come down. History, that slow child,
kept working on some infinite homework.

Restoration Elegy

'Is history deaf there, across the oceans?' Agha Shahid Ali

1

On the shore, you hear nothing above the water's
insistence, but the small clatter of pellets
extracted one by one from the child's face.
When you look back at the world: a dim car
scaling the lit highway through a canyon, window
where a hand draws a gray curtain. In the shallows,
a brown pelican resumes the last hunt of the day,
one big wing cresting the blue maw of a wave.
The swirling lift, the awkward plunge, squirming
hunger it brings up in its mouth. The quiet
after: gliding above the undertow, possessed
in the feed, as a frenzied gull lands beside it, picking
the leftover off its long yellow beak. How
they drift on the ebb, sharing this warm flesh
mauled open into blessing. Once, you saw
a mute girl say grace over dinner in a language
so heavy with hands, her face closed in a busy silence.
You knew then, the sole function of prayer was to beg
the god of oneself to stay. So in the salt of grief,
we're not forsaken, numbed by what exits our body
we're not driven to claw our faces in the dark.

2

You hear the river back home has changed
course, flooding the living rooms of your town
with its singular desire to bring to surface
every lost map of your grandfather's revolution.
In the valley, they haven't finished blinding
the children with a 12-gauge, & somewhere else
they're erasing the borders as bombsites turn green
over hurried graves. Here, the sundown flares
over the Pacific, the evening air a cross between lantana
camaras & eucalyptus, both signposts of childhood.
Like an old croon of a ghazal in praise of alcohol
remembered only in a regressing sadness now.
In the half light, walking up to your apartment,
the fog looms over the ridges, you encounter
a family of deer come down from the barren hill
to nibble on dates. At night, you hear the coyotes howl
& pray for the fawn, the only startled passenger
of the unit. No more than a few weeks old, flicking
its clean ears, as it wobbles by the bottlebrush,
not used to the stench of the animal hunger
that stops its mother still in her tracks.

Daśãi

End of the last century. None of that new money in the family yet. Only the smell of new clothes and small bills still cool from the bank vault. We're looking our best huddled in the back of a Canter the factory is letting us use for a day. Our great-grandparents are alive, giants walking the earth still. We see them once a year on this day. Later, they will go, one following the other within a month, but today, that heavy, irrevocable curtain hasn't fallen in our lives. Later, we'll tremble in our sleep, like branches of a tree whose base is grafted by an unseen hand. Then we'll all leave in directions sudden, uncharted. We'll forget the way to the homestead. But today, we're going there, swaying in the back of this truck, singing, foreheads itchy and fragrant in a pink crust of vermilion, yogurt, rice beads. This is the day that brings the branches back to seed, the blood back to the hearth. Nine goats fattened all summer were slaughtered one by one for the feast. By the time we arrive, they're simmering in a cinnamon gravy we can smell from the bend of the old school six houses away. Great-grandfather, old doctor, paces the courtyard waiting for us. His wrinkled face dappled in light pouring through palm trees. All his eight daughters come home today. Standing there, he begins to believe this will go on forever. Death is a long way off, lost on a highway somewhere, crossed a wrong border into another kingdom looking for him. A warm breeze picks up. He gazes into the bright fields. The straw-head, with his old shirt buttoned up on a stick cross, leans halfway in the shock of yellow maize.

Erato

New Delhi in Winter

Those mornings in the last days of December,
as the smog deepened over the mausoleum
& the ghost of the emperor's first wife
lingered about the four gardens, weeping
over her dead child
until a solitary jogger tore the curtain of fog
with a flashlight, making her flee
through a chink in the heavy lid of the small red tomb,
I rose at dawn, washed my face with water
cold as needles & went to work, stomach taut
as deerskin stretched over the seat of a chair.
On the terrace garden above my office,
I drank coffee & smoked a long cigarette
as something unnameable loosened its grip on my neck.
I remember thinking then, This cannot be
the worst of my days, but mostly I remember
myself in some variation of afraid.
Why, I can't tell.
I had a job, an apartment,
& a woman who claimed to be in love with me
less & less each day. The city's gray tongue
licked the windows of our room & I knew
they would come for us soon,
that one of us would be called first
to initiate the slaughter, then later
led into a dim corridor to watch
through a one-way mirror the other

slipping on entrails, trying to clamber out of it.
At the parties, I got drunk & cursed everyone.
At home, I smoked anything the women
from the university brought me.
I wrote poems that went on for years into my sleep.
When we finally parted, the city shrank
down to the few bars, her dentist, the hospital
she drove me to where they treated
the third-degree burns from the hot oil
that jumped out of a pan one night
to grab the back of my hand.
The billboards outside the malls looked
vulgar, like my scarred hand in the yellow
light that fell on the pavement. But always
that serious joy in the drunken body
stammering home in the dark.
In the daylight I felt dizzy with fear
of running into her. This vast city
open to invaders & vagrants for centuries
now small for two.
A few things became clear to me then.
The body itself has no use for hope.
It hardens in grief to live beyond hope.
And the only real use of narrative is to cheat
that ancient urge inside us, pale animal
with its face resembling the inside of our death
masks, its long unheeded, persistent murmur
clearing into a deafening verdict: Leave.

Poem with Ritual, Broken Guardrail, Imaginary Novel, & Curse

Night of liminal rain. Fall rain like a hose sluicing down the butcher's platform. This morning the high wind, sun crowning out of the double gloom, an abandoned starling nest laid bare on the treetop.

There are things I have to close before winter comes, openings, wounds like windows left unlatched in the blizzard.

Once I could prism the motherlode to a single point of devotion, meatbone of love and long hair, the thick strobelight of ardor fracturing back towards a single source.   Now I have to write the warmth back into my hands, my talons want the grip of things old.   Now things lie diffused on the earth but from a great height

you begin to see something.

When I came down from the mountains, I was changed. I loved her, but without the madness. Her body cold against me, I insisted she stay in bed a little longer.   I resented her but knew the blue arm of frost was all mine, growing inside me. I'd seen too much.

Sucked on broken spears from frozen waterfalls when stranded in thirst, seen black bears bounding the trails when it grew dark. I'd seen a village direct the evil of men through capricious deities.   Time must be named, I told her   its stochastic nature shaped in the ritual of utterance—   *I didn't sign up for this,* she said

and drove away. That night, she totaled her rage against a broken guardrail   the car bonnet caved into her chest.
I let the fact of her go then

Wrote the great unforgiving tale   from the wreck—

Found narrative, white root translucence drinking every animal trajectory of me. In improvisation, I couldn't see myself. I simulated an intensity of death paler than her blood-rimmed face of survival in the hospital bed. The way you discover a new word and see it everywhere, something followed me that was formal, observant ... followed my protagonist home into the abandoned tea estate. I made him wait there with his minor grief. Left him in the vortex of that town

where the soldiers had moved in, making the clubhouse their barracks. Left him where the dead of the town were beginning to talk through a little girl broadcasting first the ghost of the last British planter in town who fell in love with a local woman and was lynched outside the factory in the fifties

here lie the bones of the deceased
who tried to hurry the unhurrying east

And the girl?

She was from our forefathers' origin tales.

Centuries ago in the mountain village where the clan first named this curse that would follow them back one day in a town under siege, a little girl laughed under a full moon and jumped

into a vat of boiling milk.

Dissociative Love Poem

'... in whom my son already stirred' Salvatore Quasimodo

Fear like a black dog chained to a fraying post
In the stormed backyard of your brain, all night
We held ourselves like windows in a blizzard.
Mornings we were made of mist and rain.
I drank glad from your mouth some dark

Song fated to be oraled into our children's blood.
We said we would wait until the scythe fell
Two generations down by way of matricide,
Murder, or incest. We are nothing but
A sum of our history of shame. Grandfather rising

From a ditch, blood-washed face bloated purple,
Single pulse beating behind ear, left to bleed out
By the man who married his only sister—
That's as far as we talk about in the family.
How can these butchers help, you say.

Two lineages of raving bloodlines shook hands
To patch me into the world. It's true when you speak
You arrive a split second later from a farther place.
Mute shore where a child with graying hair
Stands facing a steel blue storm, waiting.

There's a two-headed God inside us all—
In you both are awake & to each other strange.

I'm walking again through a long hallway,
Rows and rows of hard, starch-white beds.
It resembles a dormitory I lived in as a schoolboy.

Half-asleep children claw at something heavy
Squatting on their chests. They heave
And writhe in some unfinished war.
I walk towards each, lean my face
To ease their gray foreheads to sleep. I stand

Before a little boy, wet and wide awake:
Your drawn-on full lips, my eyes.
He's counting on us to change our minds.

Nekyia

It is about the dead returning. A pony-tailed priest, white-haired, buttoned up in a black cassock, unravels to the camera the exact time of his death. The next moment, as it happens in dreams, I am one of them. But for a second I am both, the one watching the show & another who has returned. Then the impressions separate & fold away. I begin to check my vitals the moment I arrive. The urgent question of How do I tell myself apart from the living. The one condition that afflicts the ones who have come back seems to be an all-consuming feeling of something terminal & finished inside. A tangible bleakness mounting with an irretrievable finality, something inside your soul crouched so hard it refuses to sit up, even if you were to beat it into submission. I look around the alleyways, the schoolyard: herds of the dead have come back all at once. In gray uniforms the students walk in clumps, arms around each other, laughing, making a bullying racket. There's the burnt bride, the alcoholic who drowned face down in a ditch, the teenage girl who guttered down a pint of phenyl, all stained with recent tears. This town, it dawns on me, is in fact not my town at all. The dead accept & amplify any small familiarity. Only the women peek through windows, curious to get a glimpse of something—I can't tell what. The men look visibly embarrassed to be back. With dreary arms, they walk huddled through the streets to the market square, hunched in the cold wind, staring only at their feet going one in front of the other. Someone has told them to congregate here. Now here, they await instructions. The day is dimly lit by the shadow of a blown-out sun.

The Intelligence of Hunger

The homeless outside their bright tents
camped on the pavement along Cesar Chavez pouring
water over their napes in the heat. A brush fire
spread down the barren hills that afternoon, greasy
orange glow across the LA skyline. A small poem
gets written in our sleep beneath the din
of enormous questions stomping the streets.
As a child I slept through earthquakes, gunfire,
slept through the wailing of grown men
flogged in the youth clubs taken over by the troops.
The herd of elephants maddened with hunger
marched our streets by night, foraging the alleys
in the blind, then returned to the forest before dawn.
Where I live now every sound I make is a half-note
of loss. The bare mountain withstands, drought-
ridden, the Pacific breaking froth at its feet.
The wind rasps through the chaparral & I think
of the fire followers waiting in their late style
of hunger. The giant coreopsis that will bloom
for three bright weeks in April. I wanted to write
about these. If not love. Wildflowers, not grief.
Thirst in the shape of a deer come down from the canyon
to browse on wet grass as the sprinklers go off
at sundown. But everything here leads me
to the man they found inside the gutted Chevy
on his driveway the morning after, the fire still
raging down parts of Lost Valley, the wire

of his hands fastened to the wheel, body arched
backward into the cindered upholstery. I kept thinking
for some reason, he must have tried to wait it out
on the porch. Watching the flames leap downhill
like it was running away from itself, trying
to douse itself in shadow, dirt & bramble.
And the man, at first, must have felt a kind of pity
for its widening mouth coming down slow
to make a dry & sudden feast of where he stood,
on that deck his father once hammered to the ground.

Raidāk River, Thimphu

Wind braiding through pine

On a fog-rimmed cliff I faced the abysmal
green and pissed into the breeze

Stranded halfway to the capital
in a foreign country our jalopy an 800 Maruti
fumed from the bonnet the fan belt
combusting in a jet black foul

Long aerial notes
heaving through each needle until
the conifers swell with a low sibilant
underroar

In my language there is a name for this music
this shape this *integritas*

But standing there the dusk and the gray
fog gulfing in
I shivered and couldn't remember a thing

When we made it to the city that night
tired as drunken truckers who fall
asleep forehead on the wheel as they pull
into the grimy harbor of the border town at dusk
we only wanted to drink

On the shore
        our bare feet feeling through the sun-
warmed boulders we came
                                        before a thrumming river

                  In the dark its only form the flowing

Someone lit up something we could smoke
relieved sleek-throated bottles

                  Then the night air descended like a caul

          Above us, a heavy lid
slid out of place: the moon
                                              fell a bright column

Not on the long water
but on the blanched foreheads of my friends

          where I read something

Monstrous old familiar something
dragged by the hair   come back
bright   undisguised
come back as *itself*

It leaped across my chest

                      a black groundswell of blood
                  moving

[ ]

stance of war as a way of peacekeeping I said
remarking on the territorial habits of howler monkeys
then we each thought about distance the moon
& how warm it was you should know this
was the mid-end of winter upstate February when
grass is beginning to wake in the faint hopegreen
the crocuses rousing formless purple intent under-
soil the earth preparing halfheartedly for the lake
isn't done weaving the quilt of snow & there may be one more
instance an infant freezes to death on someone's porch & this
is how violence enters a poem through a screen
door crawling out & Mother asleep on the couch
& now it's too late I only wanted to talk
about the stance of distance as a way of timekeeping
how I'll keep finding a way to arrive in the break of cold
earth with clotty stumps I have never seen
a man fall dead & when the friend drowned at age nine
he just drowned out of sight his clothes & the yin-yang
necklace & the Casio wristwatch on the warm boulders he was
chewing on some berries & it was the quietest wade
into the underworld we waited on the shore till it got dark
when it started to rain we put our clothes on I remember
one of us sang all the way home

Toward Some Dark

They came at dawn, three angels
in jumpsuits, & felled the two ash trees
in front of the neighbor's house.

Now from our porch the view
of the sky stretched, a blue rent open
from a mesh of shadowgreen.

The scent of pine in the air, thick.
I thought this is how we arrive
at clarity. Through some clearing

of the living. When Grandfather was dying,
we found the money he'd squirreled away
in a tin box, too embarrassed to bequeath it

to any of us. Him pleading through
the final hours to please pull the fucking shroud
off his head. It was the yellow mosquito

net hung low above the bed
where he lay hallucinating, furious
we were trying to ease him toward some dark.

Our flushed faces to him then
like the inhospitable cities of his youth.
So much loss manufactured by men alone,

so why not those angels at dawn
armed with their power saws putting
simple terror back into things.

Like the monsoons bringing the abattoirs
to the flooded city streets in Dhaka.
The blinded child who asked,

Excuse me, is your Lord counting
all unrequited airstrikes? Or is
His jurassic desire our extermination to be

Now the wind flits on our porch like a young
unremembered thing, that one-legged
boy I once saw hopping across the platform

to catch the Intercity, so he could beg
through the bogies, seven stations & back.
But don't forget the wind, it has lost something

& doesn't know it, sniffing about
the heady stink of sawdust & brine, stamping
on our roof again & again

like it has stepped on so much blood
drying small wounds.

Grief Deer

Recrimination Fugue

1

So that I thought the honourable thing

After they pumped out of her stomach

Three months' worth mushed wet ball

Of crushed pills was to make a feeble exit.

Once death's veil shrivels in flames

Not even a god can utter a sentence back.

Once you crawl white-eyed through a field

Of bones into light, what happens next?

Do you sleep? Like that man who lived

In a weeping fig tree after the bombings,

I had been irresponsible with metaphor.

She wrote *The first I saw myself*

A flickering terror in my father's eyes—

A heliotrope turned away from the sun.

2

I dragged our sorrow like a hot spoor
Alone under the new city gloaming.
The doctor said grief is a hill & of guilt
A wall tonguing the bruised sky. I tried
To slap this flay back on, pronounce
The void comrade. But nights, I roused
Myself sobbing, jaws clenched mouth dry
Brain broadcasting a horror vacui
& each night, my mother her envoi:
Gone by her own hand—In a dream
She met my dead grandfather in a long
Field of snow. Faceless, he handed her
A blank paper to give me, the margin read:
This is an empty page you will never write in

3

I wanted to be both the hunger & the clarity
Gnawing each other in a white devotion.
Not this phantom limb grasping the helve
Of an axe, when for months they swept
The ground hollow beneath me. I carried
This ruin on my back across continents,
Lit vestibules, through a burning fuselage.
Like my mother bent, mending on my wet
Face what she'd marred with a shoe heel:
A foul word blooming into a swollen lip.
Nothing scared me more than children's sorrow.
Always astonished by birth's medieval show
I still wanted a daughter. My blood sprung
Whole & limbic on this ruin when I cease.

4

But on this earth, she stood nominal
And I a messenger from afar arriving first.
I played it long, unrehearsed in the charge
Sharpened my horns against the gore
Until one day half of me split to tunnel
A way out, to hammer something vestigial.
When the white gloves came on, the glow
I'd been drinking from the flask to tune back
The bile grew non-permissible. Inside
My head: *to join her back to light—*
She who loved the shape of my hands wished
Them to revise the limbo, sieve distances from
Her childhood where keening across a bed
A wake of vultures stood vigil all night.

5

But who can say there wasn't love.

Maybe love is just a lover's small intent

Listening to the cold crucible kibbling

Fire inside the beloved's skull. Nights,

I dreamt of tearing the hives unguent,

Daylight saw me tweezing stingers

From her nape. Some things I will

Always remember. Her absolute love,

Her small mouth drinking to live, the shut

Womb of her mind. Taste of her body far

Like rust, old hunger, rice strewn in milk.

With her, I thought my body inapplicable

To the world, my skin limned as backlit sheet

Where her deities shadowed into dance.

Grief Deer

who out of the tide of good flesh & long
days' steady water came sheening—
what old hound plugging the civet
of a small mammal nimble & lactating
dark teat distended mewling inside
him blind all along now sight-struck
spawning recriminations which were whip
hands lashing him hog-tied to the same
pole he used to push the boat across
the river of black froth. he had only
one chance to escape this cycle of blight
stave his limbs into the spokes fraying
cords where hands make obsolete
anyone's need to beggar a devotion

Bird of Passage

(With a line from Marlowe's grave)

Song heard when remembered—days when birds
come back—a cardinal song—on the green lip
of spring—that boy who disappeared inside his body—a will
to clasp—whom—whose white knuckle fade
bruise—synonyms for words we fill around each other—
love's formal tectonics—now silence of the cut
branch growing full straight—every morning my lover woke
there was bruise—a ceasing of grasp—the evidence of—
some white-fisted god—gag-bound sacked
on the autumn floor of her mind—threshold of pale
skin & long hair—Consider anyone wants it gets it
right—black relief against the chalk outline
of the one life you were given—finds it seemingly
endless like a scroll—a finding?—a feeling through
the folding back—easy to be snatched—away from
a plateau liminal—pause between stasis & katabasis—flatline
& orpheus—a motel called Linger—doubt or impatience
which made him turn?—Sita's black hair left out of the ground—
a continuity error—after the landmaw swallowed her—my lover
turned a pillar of salt—starch-white hospital sheet beneath—weak
ghost of abandon—endless boredom—how do you sleep—
after the white neck of slumber beneath your feet

Mezza Voce

All summer the half voice lurked behind me

& I played deaf for days for to live

To not write about it to use my body

Part the river's flesh to operate

Machinery is human too to love

& for once stay awake through it all.

Now it comes like the deer sleeved

Out of the green in clean staccato

All corpuscle & hunger—No, not the deer

The ravens calling for the wolves to split

Open the light from the dead deer's belly

Jeweled in the dark purse of its pelt.

We are each given heaven for brief so heavy

We put it down dance small around it.

NOTES

Notes, references, and inspirations for the poems in the book can be found online at www.rohanchhetri.com/notes-transit.

Acknowledgments

My sincere thanks to the editors, readers and staff of the following publications for first acknowledging the poems in this book, sometimes in different versions:

The Paris Review: Mezza Voce; King's Feedery; New Delhi in Winter

New England Review: The Indian Railway Canticle; Bordersong

Conduit: [ ]

TriQuarterly: Father, Farther: 1986

Lit Hub: National Grief

Wildness: Toward Some Dark

VINYL: Restoration Elegy

Southern Humanities Review: Lamentation for a Failed Revolution

AGNI: The Singing Bone

Corresponding Voices (11): Fish Cross the Border in Rain; Poem with Ritual, Broken Guardrail, Imaginary Novel, and Curse; Raidāk River, Thimphu; Daśāi

Jurassic Desire, a micro chapbook containing some of these poems was awarded the inaugural Per Diem Prize and was published by Per Diem Press in 2018. 'Mezza Voce' was reprinted in *Plume*. 'Toward Some Dark' was featured in the Poetry Society of America website. 'Lamentation for a Failed Revolution' was the runner-up for the Auburn Witness Poetry Prize 2018, chosen by Camille T. Dungy, and was republished in *Witness: The Red River*

Book of Poetry of Dissent (Red River, 2021). 'Fish Cross the Border in Rain' was published in *Open Your Eyes: An Anthology on Climate Change* (Hawakal, 2020). Some of these poems also appeared in the anthologies *Map Called Home* (Kitaab, 2018) and *Modern English Poetry by Younger Indians* (Sahitya Akademi, 2019).

In gratitude: My parents, Ashok Chhetri and Kala Chhetri, to whom I owe my life and mind and to whom this book is dedicated. Bruce Smith, Michael Burkard, Mary Karr, Hayan Charara, Kevin Prufer, Vivek Narayanan, Victor Hernandez, Samir Alam, Emilie Griffin, my brother Ankeet Poudel, the late Meena Alexander, Kristjan Meikop, Ishita Bal, Medha Singh, Divya Nadkarni, Sohini Basak (my editor at HarperCollins) and the readers for the 2018 Kundiman Poetry Prize. Their love, patience and support, and their suggestions and various insights at different points during the writing of this book have steered these poems toward their best versions over the years and finally into what you now hold in your hands. Special thanks to my dearest friend and 'in-house' editor Kaitlin Rizzo, whose edits in the final stages of the book were tremendously important. The fellowships from Norman Mailer Centre, Inprint Houston, and Kundiman for offering me time, resources, mentorship, and valuable friendships. Finally, I would be remiss if I did not invoke the dead writers, and some alive, without whom this book would not have been written. I hope they flicker and make themselves known to you as you move through the book.

About the Author

Rohan Chhetri is a writer and translator. He is the author of *Slow Startle* (Winner of the Emerging Poets Prize 2015). A recipient of a 2021 PEN/Heim Grant for translation, his poems have appeared in *The Paris Review*, *Revue Europe*, *AGNI* and *New England Review*, and have been translated into Greek and French.